Butterflies for Kids

by E. Jaediker Norsgaard
illustrated by John F. McGee

NorthWord Press
Minnetonka, Minnesota

WILDLIFE *For Kids* SERIES ™

Photography © 1996: Dembinsky Photo Associates: Sharon Cummings: Cover, 7, 10, 31, 40, 48;
Skip Moody: 3, 28, 32, 39; Gary Meszaros: 8, 29; Rod Planck: 17, 18, 38, 45; John Gerlach: 25.
Minden Pictures/Jim Brandenburg: 6, 34, 41. Minden Pictures/Frans Lanting: 24, 33. Frank
Oberle: 43, back cover. John Shaw: 16, 20, 22, 23, 44. Richard Hamilton Smith: 12-13.
The Wildlife Collection: Clay Myers: 27.

CREATIVE
PUBLISHING
international

NorthWord Press
5900 Green Oak Drive
Minnetonka, MN 55343
1-800-328-3895

Illustrations by John F. McGee
Book design by Lisa Moore

National Wildlife Federation® is the nation's largest conservation, education and advocacy organization.
Since 1936, NWF has educated people from all walks of life to protect nature, wildlife and the world we all share.

Ranger Rick® is an exciting magazine published monthly by National Wildlife Federation® about wildlife, nature
and the environment for kids ages 7 to 12. For more information about how to subscribe to this magazine, write:
National Wildlife Federation, 8925 Leesburg Pike, Vienna, Virginia 22184.

NWF's World Wide Web Site www.nwf.org provides instant computer access to information about
National Wildlife Federation, conservation issues and ideas for getting involved in protecting our world.

Library of Congress Cataloging-in-Publication Data

Norsgaard, E. Jaediker
Butterflies for Kids / by E. Jaediker Norsgaard.
p.   cm.
Summary: Follows two children as they raise butterflies from eggs, describing
each step of the insect's life cycle.
ISBN 1-55971-546-4 (sc)
1. Butterflies--juvenile literature. 2. Butterflies--Life cycles--Juvenile literature.
[Butterflies. 2. Caterpillars.
3. Metamorphosis.] I. Title.
QL544.2.N67 1996
595.78'9--dc20   95-36453

Printed in Malaysia

Butterflies for Kids

Tiger Swallowtail butterfly

by E. Jaediker Norsgaard
illustrated by John F. McGee

During the summer we raised butterflies we were living in a big, old farm house. The lawn was neat and trimmed, except in the backyard where we let everything grow wild.

There were more wildflowers than you could count—and where there are flowers, there are butterflies!

Butterflies are valuable pollinators. They each have a long, sucking tube called a proboscis (pronounced PRO-BO-SIS). With their proboscis they can reach deep into flowers for the sweet nectar that other pollinators can't reach.

I'm Heather and my dad is a nature film-maker. That summer he was filming the life cycles of butterflies. One sunny spring morning he took me on a butterfly egg hunt. My friend Donald joined us. He lived in the house next door.

Monarch butterfly egg

Donald was surprised to discover that butterflies start out as eggs. Dad said that most people never get to see the eggs—they're as tiny as a pinhead and have a variety of shapes. Some may be round and smooth, others are cone-shaped and have ridges. Female butterflies lay them only on the plants their larvas will eat.

Larvas are the creatures that hatch out of the eggs. But you probably know them by a different name—caterpillars. Caterpillars are very fussy about which plants they eat.

Monarch butterfly

Red Admiral butterfly

On our hunt that morning, we saw a Red Admiral butterfly. She was brown and about two-inches long. She had an orange band across her front wings and on the edges (called margins) of her hind wings.

We knew she was female since she was laying eggs on some nettles. We stayed away because nettles have hairy, stinging leaves. But Red Admiral caterpillars like to feed on them. They also eat the vine-like leaves of plants called hops. These caterpillars have spines that stick out, probably to scare predators away.

Red Admiral caterpillars do something interesting to shelter themselves. They pull the leaves of the plant together and bind them closed with silk.

In winter, the adult Red Admiral butterflies also hibernate this way.

We walked through our backyard to a nearby meadow where something caught my eye. It was a bright brown Buckeye butterfly. The Buckeye had some orange markings and large eye spots on the upper sides of its hind and front wings. I could see that its underside was lighter.

Dad told us that their spiny caterpillars feed on plantain and gerardia plants. Sometimes these butterflies migrate south for the winter.

Buckeye butterfly

Many stalks of broad-leafed milkweed grew in the meadow. Dad showed us how to examine the under-side of a milkweed leaf to see if a Monarch butterfly had laid one of her hundreds of eggs there.

Even though she has to lay so many eggs, she usually only puts one on a leaf. This way she can be sure that some will survive.

I thought I found one but it turned out to be a drop of white milkweed juice. I knew that wouldn't hatch!

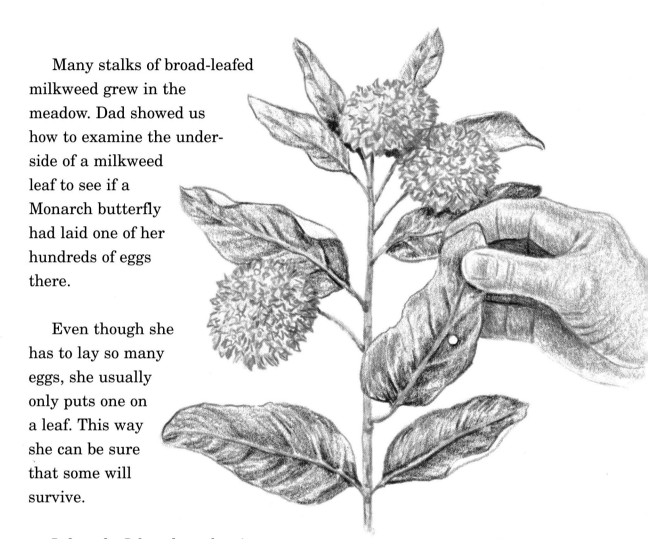

Then Donald saw an orange Monarch flying from leaf to leaf. We followed her to where she laid an egg, keeping our distance.

With a scissors, Dad cut a few inches of leaf around each egg. I asked him if the butterfly mother would be upset to see us taking her eggs. He said not to worry, after she lays them she moves on—her mission is accomplished. She doesn't need to stay around and teach her larvas anything . . . they're born knowing exactly what to do.

We brought fifteen Monarch eggs home. Mom gave us a foil tray and Dad lined it with a damp paper towel before placing the eggs on it. He said the towel was to keep the leaves from drying out. Then he showed us how to wrap a clear plastic bag loosely around the tray to help keep the leaves fresh. He gave Donald a couple of eggs to raise at his house.

Monarch butterfly

Each day we checked the tray with a magnifying glass, looking for any action. On the fourth day I saw a black dot at the tip of each ribbed, cone-shaped egg. The black dots were the heads of the baby caterpillars!

Soon, one poked its head through a hole that it ate in its "eggshell," and the others soon did the same. After eating the shell, the larva began nibbling tiny holes in the leaves. It was hard to believe that this almost invisible little thing would soon become a butterfly!

Donald was upset because his eggs didn't hatch. We found out that his house was too cold for them because it was air-conditioned. So he helped raise mine.

In a few days the caterpillars were twice as big. They were still pretty tiny, but you could see yellow, white, and black stripes around their bodies. They spent most of their time eating and growing. Donald and I were in charge of keeping them supplied with fresh milkweed leaves.

Monarch butterfly caterpillar

After about a week, we moved the caterpillars to a screened cage where they had more room to move around. It had a wood frame and was about 14 inches square. We stuck a whole stem of milkweed leaves in a jar of water and put it in the cage.

While gathering the leaves, we saw a beautiful Comma butterfly. It was about two inches long and orange brown with black markings. It's called an angle-winged butterfly. That's because of the sharp angles that give its wings a raggedy appearance. Its caterpillars feed on nettle and hops, just like the Red Admiral's.

Comma butterfly

We had lots of fun in the days that followed searching for butterflies and trying to identify them. We saw some little American Copper butterflies that were only about an inch wide. They had a metallic coppery luster that made them glimmer in the sunlight.

American Copper butterfly

American Copper butterfly caterpillars eat sheep sorrel plants and spend the winter on them as pupas, the stage between caterpillar and butterfly.

We realized that different kinds of butterflies have adapted in different ways, according to the change of seasons. We also figured out that most butterflies couldn't live without the plants that people call weeds!

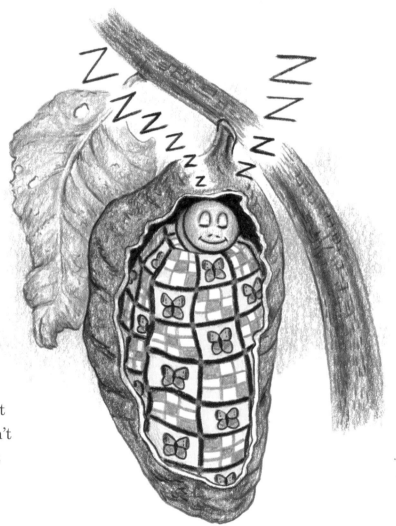

Monarch butterfly

About two weeks after they hatched, when the Monarch caterpillars were two inches long, they stopped eating—which was fine with me because I was the one who had to change the paper full of their round black droppings at the bottom of their cage.

"Look Heather. They're restless," Donald said as he watched them. He was right, the caterpillars were wandering around the cage.

"They're ready to go into the next stage of their metamorphosis," Dad said. Metamorphosis (MET-A-MOR-FO-SIS) is a Greek word meaning "change of form." This was what we were really excited to see—these worm-like, crawling caterpillars becoming butterflies with wings.

Dad put several twigs with horizontal branches in the cage. The caterpillars crawled over them and seemed to be searching for just the right spot to hang themselves upside-down and go into their pupa stage.

Donald and I looked at them closely, expecting a caterpillar to pick its spot at any minute. We watched and waited that whole day but nothing happened.

The next day, a Monarch caterpillar selected a spot and started weaving a little silk button from a tube, called a spinneret, in its lower lip. It didn't seem to be in any hurry. Finally, after attaching its two rear legs to the silk, its remaining legs loosened their grip on the twig very slowly until the caterpillar was hanging head down.

Pretty soon all the caterpillars were hanging peacefully, their long black feelers limp. With their necks curved, they each looked like a little letter J.

Monarch butterfly caterpillar

We had to wait until the next day before each hanging caterpillar was ready to transform itself into a chrysalis (KRIS-AH-LIS). They had wriggled out of their skins several times before. It's a process called molting and they have to do it because the skin doesn't grow larger as they grow. Each time they shed their old skin, a new one is underneath.

Now they were going to peel their skins off for the last time and we weren't sure what was underneath.

Each caterpillar kept stretching again and again until the skin split behind its neck and along its back. The rippling movements pushed the skin upward. And underneath was just a soft, green blob!

"Watch carefully, Heather," Dad said. "Each one must work very hard to hook a little stem at the end of its abdomen into the silk button, before detaching its skin and throwing it away. If it can't hook its abdomen into the silk, it'll fall down and die. And it can't even see what it's doing upside-down!"

Monarch butterfly pupa

Monarch butterfly chrysalises

We were relieved when they all made it. In just an hour the green blobs became harder and smoother. Later, little dots appeared that shone like gold. Yesterday they were caterpillars and today they looked like jade-green charms. Tempting as it was, we didn't touch the chrysalises. We didn't want to hurt them.

They hung that way for between 9 and 14 days. Although they seemed to be doing nothing, we knew they were very busy growing inside.

During the days we were waiting for the butterflies to come out of their chrysalises, we tried to see how many different kinds of butterflies we could find outside.

The biggest one we saw was a 3-inch Great Spangled Fritillary fluttering around our wildflowers. It had dark spots and wavy lines on its orange wings and the underside was spotted with silver. Its spiny caterpillars hibernate soon after hatching. They wake up in the spring and feed at night, mostly on violets.

I was glad that the lawns around the house were dotted with little purple violets in the spring. Maybe we would have more Fritillaries next year!

Great Spangled Fritillary butterfly

One afternoon, Donald called me into the backyard. A large, black-striped, yellow Tiger Swallowtail butterfly was sipping nectar from the dahlia flowers that were planted around our bird bath. What a beautiful sight! These caterpillars have false eye spots that may frighten away predators like birds. They feed on hops, willow, poplar, wild cherry and tuliptrees, depending on where they live.

Tiger Swallowtail butterfly caterpillar

Black Swallowtail butterfly

Dad asked if we wanted to raise some Black Swallowtails while our Monarchs were still in their chrysalises. We sure did! I liked looking for their single round yellow eggs on the thin green stems under Queen Anne's Lace flowers. I also found some on parsley and carrot leaves.

Dad put some of the flowers with their leaves and the eggs on a few inches of sand in a jumbo size glass jar. We covered the jar with gauze so they would have plenty of air. The eggs hatched five days later. At first the baby caterpillars were dark with white marks shaped like saddles, but as they grew they turned green with yellow-dotted black bands.

Donald picked one up and it thrust out something that looked like a thorn from behind its head. It was really a small, forked, orange scent gland that gave off a stinky smell. He quickly put it back in the jar.

While we were picking fresh Queen Anne's Lace leaves for our caterpillars to eat, we noticed a Spicebush Swallowtail butterfly. It looked a little like the Black Swallowtails, dark with greenish hind wings. The females are more blue than green. Their caterpillars also have false eye spots, and eat spicebush and sassafras.

Spicebush Swallowtail butterfly

In about two weeks our Black Swallowtail caterpillars were ready to transform into chrysalises. Dad stuck a few straight sticks into the sand at an angle.

Donald and I thought we knew what to expect next, but were we surprised!

Instead of hanging themselves upside down like the Monarchs, they attached their hind legs to the stick and stood straight up. They wove a safety belt of silk to support themselves, like window washers outside a tall building.

The next day, their skin split down their backs. This was very tricky to do because they had to detach their rear ends from the silk button and hang for a second, held only by the safety belt. Then they had to bring a stem on their body, called a cremaster (KREE-MAS-TER), around the skin and fasten it into the silk button before dropping the skin.

Now they were chrysalises. But they didn't look like green charms like the Monarchs did. They looked more like long, pearly green and brown sea shells. They still had their safety belts around them. It would be about 12 days before they emerged as butterflies.

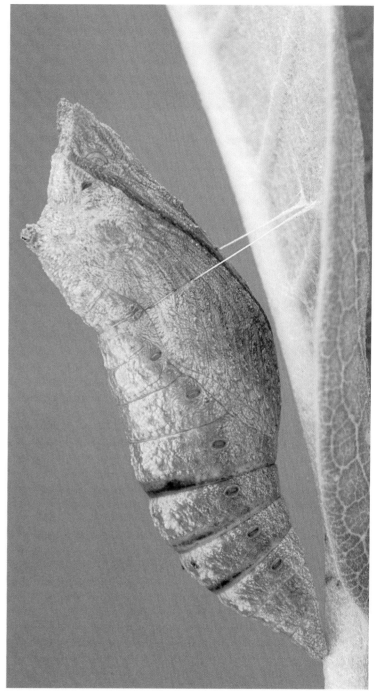

Black Swallowtail butterfly pupa

I wanted to know how we could tell when the Monarch butterflies would be ready to emerge from their chrysalises. Dad said that about one and a half days before, you can see the chrysalis change from jade green to teal blue, and gradually darken. About twelve hours later it becomes transparent enough to see the orange wings folded up inside.

One by one, the chrysalises turned frosty as the butterfly moved inside. Suddenly the seams started cracking, and all at once it opened. The butterfly tumbled out and clung to the empty shell with its long legs.

Monarch butterfly chrysalis

It was still small and crinkled but I could see the muscles pumping blood into the black veins in its wings. Soon the butterfly expanded to full size, about 3 inches across.

The caterpillar had changed into a totally different creature . . . it seemed like a miracle.

The wings had to dry before the butterfly could fly, and it had to connect the two halves of its long black proboscis, or else it wouldn't be able to drink. We watched it coil and uncoil the proboscis until it was working.

New Monarch butterfly

Monarch butterfly wing

When Donald came over, the butterfly was still clinging to its shell. We looked at the orange and black wings through a magnifying glass. They had tiny scales, and all together they looked like velvet. A butterfly's scientific name is Lepidoptera. It means "scale-winged" in Greek. Moths are Lepidopteras too.

When the Monarch opened its wings, we saw a small black dot on each hind wing that marks the male scent glands—so this butterfly was a boy! The scent glands are used to attract female Monarchs.

By the next afternoon, all the Monarchs had emerged. We were eager to set them free, but it rained for two days so we couldn't just yet. They can't fly when their wings are wet or too cold, so you see them flying mostly on warm sunny days.

To keep them fed until they could drink the nectar of flowers, we mixed some water and honey in a saucer and carefully placed it in the cage. Each butterfly uncoiled its proboscis and sipped the sweet liquid—just like we sip soda pop through a straw.

When the sun finally came out, we opened the cage in the backyard. A few of the Monarchs flew high and circled overhead. Most flew to nearby flowers or landed in the trees.

One of the butterflies was already pollinating flowers, although it probably didn't know it. On a flower, grains of pollen stuck to the butterfly's proboscis and rubbed off on the next flower it visited, fertilizing the seeds so new plants would grow.

I knew that Monarchs usually fly south for the winter. But Dad said these Monarchs weren't going to migrate. Our butterflies would mate and lay eggs, maybe even in our backyard. But the eggs these Monarchs laid would hatch in late summer or fall, and the new butterflies would fly thousands of miles to spend the winter in Mexico or California. Imagine those fragile-looking wings flying so far!

We hoped our butterflies would not stop at gardens where weed killers and other pesticides had been sprayed. Some people don't understand how hazardous the poisons are to all living things. That's the main reason butterfly populations keep decreasing.

Painted Lady butterfly

After our butterflies flew away, we saw a Painted Lady butterfly flying around some tall purple thistles. We walked closer and saw splashes of orange and dark brown with white spots on its front wings. It was only about two inches across. When it landed we could see five small eye spots on the underside of each hind wing.

Later, we went back to the same spot to see if any Painted Lady butterfly caterpillars were feeding on the prickly leaves. The caterpillars have short spines sticking out of their bodies. They make shelters of leaf bits held together with silk. That ability to produce silk thread sure is a handy thing to have!

The American Painted Lady is also called Hunter's butterfly. It looks like the Painted Lady, but has two large eye spots on the underside of the hind wings.

American Painted Lady butterfly

Viceroy butterfly

    We ran toward what we thought was one of our Monarchs. But this one had a thin black line across each hind wing. It turned out to be a Viceroy. They mimic the Monarch's looks. That helps protect them from animals that might otherwise eat them. Monarchs have an unpleasant taste from the milkweed they eat, so hardly anything eats Monarchs.

Monarch butterflies

It seemed like a long 12 days before our Black Swallowtail butterflies finally emerged from their chrysalises. The Swallowtails climbed up on the sticks while their wings expanded and dried. With wings open, the butterflies were about 3 inches wide.

I was glad it was still early enough in the season for them to come out. Had it been later, though, they would have spent the whole winter as chrysalises and not emerged until spring.

Black Swallowtail butterfly

Checkered Skipper butterfly

After releasing them, we walked to a nearby pond and saw lots of small brown and white Checkered Skipper butterflies. There are more than 2,000 kinds of Skippers! They have thick, moth-like bodies and little curved clubs at the ends of their antennas. These were at the pond because their larvas feed on mallow plants that grow there.

Later that summer, when the lavender asters bloomed, light brownish Pearl Crescent butterflies appeared. They were tiny—only 1-1/2 inches across. Their eggs are laid in clusters on the asters and the caterpillars stay together, feeding in a group.

Pearl Crescent butterfly

Donald and I raised another, larger batch of Monarchs that summer and had to walk to a field nearby to find enough milkweed to feed them. Somehow, a few of the caterpillars must have escaped from their cage when I was changing the paper. I discovered it several weeks later, when a butterfly popped out on my bed and two popped out on the curtains!

I often tried to picture our Monarchs flying south for the winter. They would join their relatives who were hanging out together in the trees by the thousands, resting until winter's end.

Black Swallowtail butterfly

After that wonderful summer, I smile whenever I see a Monarch or a Black Swallowtail. I always hope it's a relative of those we had so much fun raising!